CLICK, CLACK, Splish, Splash

A Counting Adventure

by doreen cronin
and
betsy lewin

atheneum books for young readers

NEW YORK LONDON TORONTO SYDNEY

For Julia
—D. C.

To Julia again, and to Grace Isabelle—
have a great childhood!
—B. L.

Visit us at www.abdopub.com

Spotlight, a division of ABDO Publishing Company, is a school and
library distributor of high quality reinforced library bound editions.

Library bound edition © 2006

Atheneum Books for Young Readers
An imprint of Simon & Schuster Children's Publishing Division
1230 Avenue of the Americas
New York, New York 10020
Text copyright © 2006 by Doreen Cronin
Illustrations copyright © 2006 by Betsy Lewin
All rights reserved, including the right of reproduction in whole or
in part in any form.
Book design by Ann Bobco
The text for this book is set in Filosofia.
The illustrations for this book are rendered in brush and watercolor.
Manufactured in the United States of America
First Edition
10 9 8 7 6 5 4 3 2 1

Library of Congress Cataloging-in-Publication Data
Cronin, Doreen.
Click, clack, splish, splash: a counting adventure / Doreen Cronin ; illustrated by Betsy
Lewin.—1st ed.
p.   cm.
Summary: While Farmer Brown sleeps, some of the animals who live on
the farm go on a fishing expedition.
ISBN-13: 978-0-689-87716-2
ISBN-10: 0-689-87716-1
1-59961-090-6 (reinforced library bound edition)
[1. Animals—Fiction. 2. Farmers—Fiction. 3. Fishing—Fiction.
4. Counting. 5. Stories in rhyme.]
I. Title: Click, clack, one two three. II. Lewin, Betsy, ill. III. Title.
PZ8.3.C879Cl 2006
[E]—dc22   2004029020

All Spotlight books are reinforced library binding and manufactured in the United States of America.

CLICK, CLACK, Splish, Splash

A Counting Adventure

by doreen cronin

and

betsy lewin

1 farmer sleeping.

2 feet creeping.

3 buckets piled high.

4 chickens
standing
by.

5 cows type a note.

6 goats load the boat.

7 pigs lead the way.

8 sheep decide to stay.

9

mice

leave

a

note

on

the

door.

All the animals

go to the shore.

10 buckets lined up in a row.

10 fish ready to go.

One sleepy farmer rubs his eyes
and wakes up to a fishy surprise!